In the Footprints of the Yeti

Stalked by Bigfoot

Two Legends About Wild, Hairy Ape-men

RETOLD BY JOANNA KORBA
ILLUSTRATED BY ADAM GUSTAVSON

Table of Contents

LEGENDS

What is a legend?

A legend is a story that has grown up around a famous figure or event. Legends are usually based on historical events, but they are fictionalized. The legend of King Arthur and the Round Table, for example, grew from stories of a warrior king who lived around 600 C.E.

What is the purpose of a legend?

Legends often tell about a person who actually lived or an event that really happened. But, like myths and fairy tales, their purpose is to tell inspiring or cautionary adventure stories about people or events that were important to a culture. They feature heroes who are strong, brave, and honest; the listeners learn good values from the actions of these heroes or the results of the events. Legends may also explain the origin of a geographical feature, such as a mountain or an ocean, or tell how a place got its name.

How do you read a legend?

Do not look for factual retellings of events or realistic portrayals of characters when you read a legend. Instead, be prepared for fantastic details and extraordinary people or creatures. Ask yourself: *What parts of the legend might be true? What parts make the legend an adventure story?*

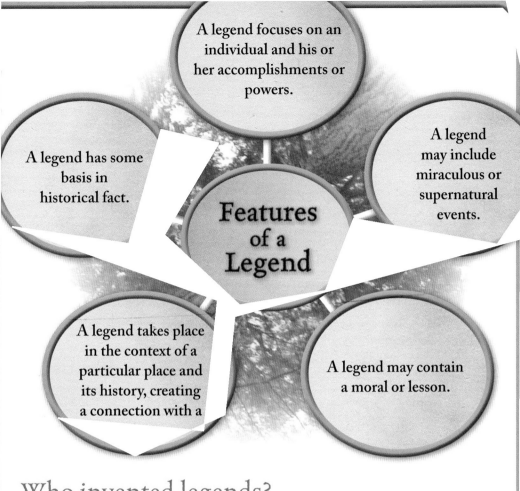

A legend focuses on an individual and his or her accomplishments or powers.

A legend has some basis in historical fact.

A legend may include miraculous or supernatural events.

Features of a Legend

A legend takes place in the context of a particular place and its history, creating a connection with a

A legend may contain a moral or lesson.

Who invented legends?

Legends are part of the oral tradition—storytellers told them to listeners who handed them down from generation to generation. Early listeners were probably familiar with the heroes of legends and already knew about their exploits. Storytellers added heroic qualities, daring deeds, and excitement to the legends.

Over the years legends grew up around characters like King Arthur and Robin Hood. Today readers enjoy legends for the same reason they always have—the excitement of a good story and the interesting characters.

Tools for Readers and Writers

MOOD

Let's say you've just read the first few pages of a legend where the setting is the wild Carpathian Mountains. The craggy land is covered with gnarled old trees where all kinds of creatures—you don't know what kind—lurk. What is out there? And do you really want to know? All of these descriptions set a creepy, suspenseful mood. Authors want their readers to experience a particular feeling as they read. That feeling, called **mood**, may be fear, anger, joy, sadness, or more. When you write, think about what you want your readers to feel.

PREFIXES

Prefixes are small letter groups added at the beginning of a base word, or root, that change the meaning of the word. Understanding prefixes and their meanings helps readers and writers build vocabulary. Beginning readers and writers use simple prefixes like *un-* and *re-*. More advanced readers and writers have a larger arsenal of prefixes. These include *omni* meaning "all" as in **omnipotent** and *dia* meaning "through or across" as in **diagonal**.

SEQUENCE OF EVENTS

Good authors write stories with events occurring in the beginning, middle, and end. These events are logically placed, creating a story's natural flow and rhythm. To help readers better understand a story's sequence, authors often include key words and phrases such as **on** (date), **not long after, finally, when, as**, and **before**. Good readers look for a story's natural progression of events to help them better understand the plot.

About these Legendary Creatures

Tales of wild ape-men are found in stories from all over the world. Two have reached legendary status: Bigfoot and the yeti (also known as the Abominable Snowman).

Bigfoot often goes by the name of Sasquatch, from the Salish (Native American) word *Saskets*, meaning "the giant." Most "sightings" are in the Pacific Northwest, though reports have been filed in every state except Hawaii about a creature from six to ten feet tall covered in dark brown or reddish-brown, shaggy hair. Bigfoot's personality is unpredictable. He may be shy and gentle, mischievous and playful, or vicious and dangerous.

One of the most famous Bigfoot tales was recounted by Theodore Roosevelt, the twenty-sixth U.S. president, in his 1892 book *The Wilderness Hunter*. He told of an old trapper's youthful encounter with a Bigfoot creature. The man, Bauman, and an unnamed companion, were trapping in the wilderness of what is now the state of Montana in the 1840s.

Tales of the yeti come from the other side of the world—the Himalayan mountains of Asia. This mountain range stretches 1,500 miles between northern India and the Tibetan Plateau in China. Nine of the ten tallest mountains are found here. When outsiders come to climb these giants or search for the yeti, they often call on the climbing skills of Sherpas. These hardy Tibetan people live mostly in Nepal, in the heart of the Himalayas.

How did the yeti get his name? Some say it comes from a Sherpa word meaning "that thing." Others argue that it is from a Tibetan name meaning "rocky bear." Descriptions of the yeti's size do not match either. He may be anywhere from four-and-a-half to sixteen feet tall, but most accounts have him over six feet. He is usually described as covered with shaggy reddish-brown or dark-brown hair, with a white ape-like face. His behavior may be shy and gentle or frightening and aggressive,

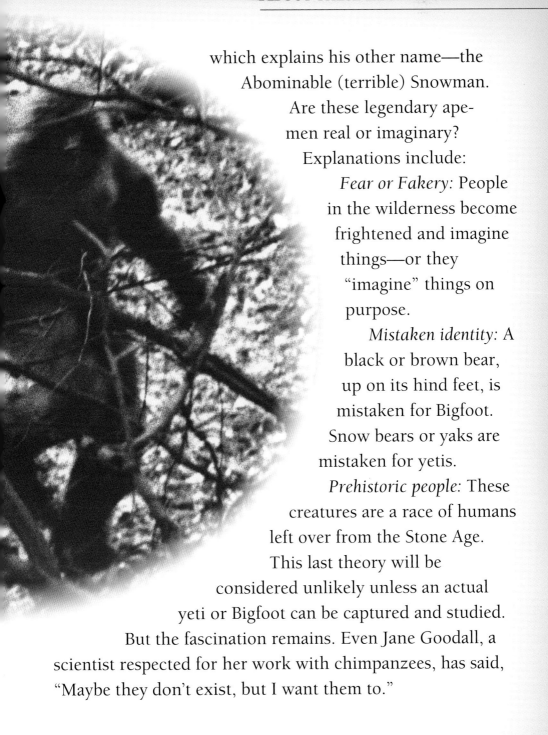

which explains his other name—the Abominable (terrible) Snowman.

Are these legendary ape-men real or imaginary? Explanations include:

Fear or Fakery: People in the wilderness become frightened and imagine things—or they "imagine" things on purpose.

Mistaken identity: A black or brown bear, up on its hind feet, is mistaken for Bigfoot. Snow bears or yaks are mistaken for yetis.

Prehistoric people: These creatures are a race of humans left over from the Stone Age.

This last theory will be considered unlikely unless an actual yeti or Bigfoot can be captured and studied. But the fascination remains. Even Jane Goodall, a scientist respected for her work with chimpanzees, has said, "Maybe they don't exist, but I want them to."

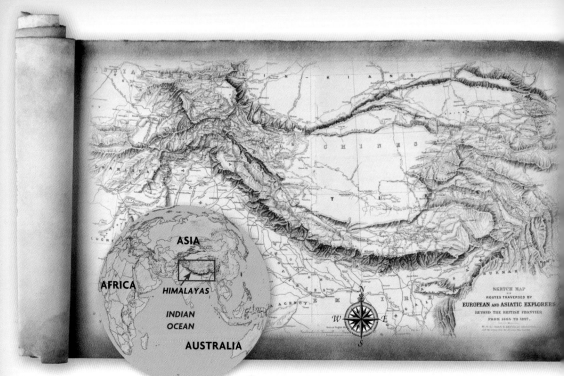

ASIA

AFRICA

HIMALAYAS

INDIAN
OCEAN

AUSTRALIA

SKETCH MAP
OF
ROUTES TRAVERSED BY
EUROPEAN AND ASIATIC EXPLORERS
BEYOND THE BRITISH FRONTIER
FROM 1865 TO 1897.

In the
Footprints OF THE
Yeti

The towering, snow-wrapped Himalayas are a forbidding place, a world of sudden avalanches, shrieking winds, and little oxygen to breathe. Who could possibly live in such desolation, up where the Earth meets the sky at the "roof of the world"?

The yetis.

Few have seen these mysterious, elusive creatures. Those who have describe yetis as tall and extremely strong, with light faces and covered with long, chestnut hair that glistens in the icy sunlight. They walk on two manlike feet and gesture with two manlike hands. They are like us and they are not like us . . . .

Over a century ago, two Englishmen encountered these otherworldly beings. The men were globe-trotting adventurers, always searching for excitement and hoping for glory. Their names have been lost to time, but let's call them Mr. Philips and Mr. Mitchell.

Their travels had led them to Kathmandu, Nepal, in the foothills of the Himalayas. They sought out the Swayamb-hunath temple, an ancient shrine that was a gathering spot in the city. Here mingled visiting pilgrims, food vendors, families having picnics, and mischievous monkeys who scampered about as they tried to snatch food out of unsuspecting hands.

The men were immediately approached by a short, sturdy, smooth-faced man. Since he was dressed in the traditional *chuba*, an ankle-length robe tied with a sash, the Englishmen correctly deduced that he was a Sherpa.

The Sherpa, in turn, had concluded by their appearance that the two were Europeans. "*Parlez-vous Français?*" he inquired. Seeing their frowns, he spoke again. "English?"

When they nodded, he spoke eagerly. "That is good. English is better than French. I am Tsering. Do you need a guide?"

"That depends," Mitchell answered. "You see, Philips and I—I'm Mitchell—we're on a hunt for some special game. We've heard tales of an amazing creature that lives in these mountains." He looked carefully at the Sherpa. "Do you know what I'm talking about?"

The Sherpa smiled and nodded. "Some say he is dangerous and call him *raksha*, demon, but others say he is kind and gentle and call him *kang admi*, snow man. You mean the yeti, do you not?"

Philips looked almost **euphoric**. "Right you are, the yeti! Can you help us find these yetis?" He glanced at Philips with a sly smile before continuing. "We would love to . . . to *observe* them."

The little man shrugged. "I can take you to a snowfield where they are sometimes seen. This does not mean you will see one. They are shy creatures."

The offer seemed to satisfy the Englishmen, and arrangements were quickly made. The three would buy provisions that day and set out early the next morning for a Tibetan Buddhist monastery partway up a nearby peak. The snowfield in question was perhaps a mile up from the monastery, over steep, snow-covered terrain.

The little expedition set out at dawn. The Sherpa was uneasy when he saw that the men had rifles in their packs, but the Englishmen quickly assured him that the guns were for safety only, in case they encountered snow bears.

The ground at that altitude was not snow-covered at that time of the year, so it was a quick hike to the mountain. The climb to the monastery was not difficult, either, although it took all morning. As the party of three passed through the gate, peace enveloped them. From the main temple they could hear the low, steady, **euphonious** chanting of the monks as they sang their prayers.

Climbing the Himalayas in the 1950s (left). A Sherpa, 1967 (right)

11

"We cannot disturb them at prayer," the Sherpa said. "We will wait in the dining hall. Now when you meet the monks, do not introduce yourselves or ask them their names," he counseled. "It is not done. Simply call each man *Kusho-la*."

Later, when the red-robed monks entered the dining hall, the Englishmen stayed back, packs out of sight, letting the Sherpa conduct the discussion in Tibetan. When the little man rejoined them, he was followed by one of the monks.

"This man speaks some English," he said. "Kusho-la, these are the Englishmen I was telling you about."

Philips looked sharply at the Sherpa. "Did you tell him we're interested in yetis?" The little man nodded, so Philips turned eagerly to the monk. "Kusho-la, are there really yetis in the snowfield near here?"

The monk smiled gently. "Yes, we have seen them there."

"Have they ever attacked you?" Mitchell asked.

The monk looked surprised. "No. Why would they? They are gentle. And they know we would never harm them."

The Englishmen nodded happily, as if they were confirming something they already knew. Then they made arrangements for the three of them to stay that afternoon and night at the monastery.

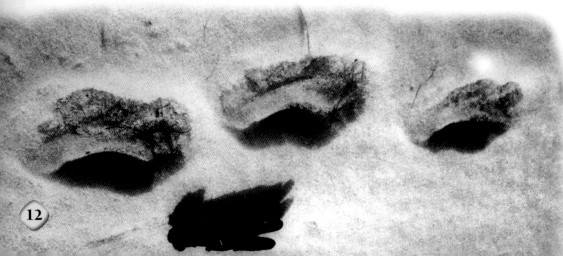

The next morning, dressed in their warmest clothes, the Englishmen set out with the Sherpa for the snowfield. Philips and Mitchell carried their rifles. Upon reaching the snowfield, they discovered many large footprints left by two-legged creatures, but they saw no yetis. The Sherpa, meanwhile, was growing increasingly suspicious of the Englishmen's true motives. When the three returned to the monastery that evening, he challenged them.

"Why did you have your guns out all the time?" he demanded. "There were no snow bears around. Why did you not have your looking-glasses with you if you wanted to *observe* the yetis."

Mitchell and Philips had decided the night before that they had no more use for Tsering. The Sherpa had served his purpose by leading them to the snowfield. They would simply return and wait until they got what they had come for. But this was not what they told the Sherpa. Instead, they apologized for being so nervous about snow bears and **hypocritically** promised to pack their guns away. They had taken a liking to the monastery, they said, and wanted to stay a few days. Then they paid Tsering for his time and parted ways.

The next morning, the Sherpa left for Kathmandu, and the Englishmen left for the snowfield. Since they intended to camp out until they killed a yeti, they took along a tent, food, and their guns. They left at dawn while the monks were at prayer.

Retracing their way to the snowfield, they spent the day examining the tracks the yetis had left. Some looked fresh, but there were no creatures to be seen that day or the next.

The men were running out of time. The lack of oxygen at that altitude was beginning to tire them out. Then, on the third day, the weather turned vicious. The wind whipped up and snow began to fall thickly. The Englishmen retreated to their tent to wait the storm out. It raged through the night, keeping them up. In the morning, they looked at one another with worried eyes.

"Should we stay put?" Mitchell asked through chattering teeth. He looked to be on the verge of **hypothermia**.

"We're both weak from lack of oxygen and dealing with the bitter cold," Philips said grimly. "And the snow will bury us before long. We've got to leave soon or not at all."

As the storm raged on, the exhausted men dozed off. Then something woke Philips. He was aware of movement and mutterings outside the tent. Carefully opening one corner of the door flap, he peered into the wind-swept snow and dimly spied three tall shapes wrapped in fur. When they saw him, one raised its arm and gestured for him to follow.

He waved back and turned to Mitchell. "Wake up, man!" he cried. "Some of the monks have come to lead us back to the monastery!"

Mitchell blinked and smiled feebly. "That's good," he said and broke into a fit of coughing.

Philips knew he would have to help Mitchell walk, so everything was left behind as the two staggered from the tent. They waded through the thick sea of snow and icy wind, weak from hunger, following behind the three shaggy shapes that led the way. Their rescuers were careful to stay just a little ways ahead, waiting patiently for the two men to follow.

Suddenly, the monastery loomed before them. At that moment, Mitchell collapsed again. When Philips got him back on his feet, he looked around for the three shaggy shapes. They were gone. But some monks were hurrying toward them, helping them into the dining hall, stripping off their wet clothes, wrapping them in warm blankets, setting them beside a roaring fire.

Later, Philips and Mitchell sought out the monk who spoke English. Philips spoke. "We wanted to thank the three monks who came to the snowfield to save us."

The monk spoke softly. "None of the monks have left the monastery since the storm began. Don't you know who saved you? I told you they were gentle."

Early the next morning, the storm stopped. Soon after, some monks went out to clear a path to the monastery gate. They came back with news. Just outside the gate sat the two Englishmen's belongings—everything they had left behind in the snowfield, in a neat pile—including their guns.

Analyze the Characters, Setting, and Plot

- Who are the main characters in the legend?
- Who are the minor characters in the legend?
- What are Philips and Mitchell after? What is their intent when they find their goal?
- How does their intent affect the Sherpa?
- What causes Philips and Mitchell to change their attitudes about yetis?
- How does the legend end?

Focus on Comprehension: Sequence of Events

- The Sherpa was uneasy about the men carrying rifles. What did the Englishmen say about this?
- The monk said that the yetis were gentle. What question from the Englishmen prompted this answer?
- What did the Englishmen do right after they saw the shaggy shapes?

Focus on Nonfiction within Fiction

Fiction authors sometimes include a nonfiction narrative in the text. Reread the first few paragraphs of this story. How does the nonfiction narrative enhance the text? What did you think about as you switched from nonfiction to fiction?

Analyze the Tools Writers Use: Mood

- In the third paragraph of the story (on page 9), what mood does the author establish when introducing the yetis? How does this mood affect your feeling toward the creatures?
- When the expedition reaches the monastery, the author creates two moods. One for the monk and one for the expedition. Describe the two moods.
- What mood is the writer trying to show with her description of the men in the tent during the storm? How do you think she wants you to feel about Phillips and Mitchell? Why is this a turning point in the story?

Focus on Words: Prefixes

Two advanced prefixes are *eu* meaning "good" and *hypo* meaning "lower than." Words that use these prefixes are **eulogy** which means "saying good things about someone" and **hypodermic** which means "under the skin." Make a chart like the one below. Read each word in the chart. Identify the part of speech of each word as it is used in the story. Finally, explain how the prefix changes the meaning of the base word.

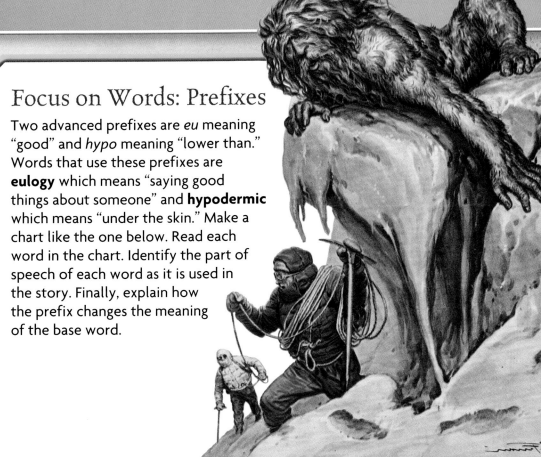

Page	Word	Part of speech	How the prefix changes the meaning of the base word
11	euphoric		
11	euphonious		
13	hypocritically		
14	hypothermia		

Stalked by Bigfoot

When this tale is told around the campfire, even brave folks find themselves looking uneasily into the surrounding darkness, wondering what might be lurking out there. Don't be surprised if you find yourself doing the same.

Well, now that you've been warned, this is the way the tale goes . . . .

MONTANA TERRITORY

B ack when America was just a young country, mostly wild, there was a young trapper named Bauman. He was an intrepid lad, unafraid of venturing into dark, lonely places your ma wouldn't want you to go. So it was that one warm, sunny morning he set out with a partner, another strapping young lad like himself, on two lean mountain ponies. These boys headed into Montana territory, carrying a load of traps, with the **expectation** of capturing beaver. They had determined to trap along the Wisdom River, as it was called then. Sure, it's got a different name now—Big Hole River—but it's still the same river.

Now, these two boys, between them, had plenty of trapping **expertise**, but they were still having no luck on that river. Not a beaver to be found. Now, it seems they had heard tell of a stream that was jam-packed with the furry little creatures. Trouble was, this particular stream was situated in a remote mountain pass inhabited by a particularly nasty beast that had taken a strong dislike to people. Wanted them all to keep out. The Indians were careful to **circumvent** the place altogether, although one white man had been fool enough to set foot in its territory—and had paid for it with his life.

The author establishes the setting of the story. Legends take place in the context of a particular culture and its history. Montana of 160 years ago was a wild, unexplored place.

the Big Hole River today

The author talks about the legendary creature of the story, whom she describes as a "nasty beast," reportedly responsible for one man's death. The reader is left wondering, *When will the creature appear?*

But these two trappers were young and eager, and **exhilarated** at the thought of all those beavers for the taking.

"Don't you worry about that nonsense that scared old redskin told us," said Bauman. "We got our rifles and courage to protect us."

So the boys rode their little ponies up to the bottom of the pass, which was too steep and rocky to manage on horseback. They left the animals beside a stream in a meadow, tied up and happily nibbling on some grass. Shouldering their gear, Bauman and his partner began the hike up to the stream.

The forest quickly closed in on them as only an old pine forest can, its tall, shaggy limbs interlocking overhead, with lances of sunlight piercing through here and there to light the way. Beneath their feet was a carpet of brown needles that crunched as they walked. The trees whispered in the wind. There were other noises too—a bird crying out over here, a chipmunk scuttling through the underbrush over there.

a Montana forest

The sun was low in the sky by the time they found a decent camping site—a little glade **circumscribed** by densely packed pines, just big enough for a patch of sunlight to warm the grassy ground. The two trappers quickly erected a lean-to beside a tiny brook, using brush and branches they found in the glade. They threw down their packs but didn't bother opening them. The partners were determined to set some traps before dusk.

Darkness was threatening by the time they returned to camp, but there was enough light left to witness the destruction that had taken place. Their lean-to had been torn to pieces. Their packs had been gutted and the contents flung about.

Must have been a bear, they figured. What else could it be?

They shrugged off their misfortune and began setting the camp to rights, gathering up their scattered gear, rebuilding their lean-to, and making a large fire. As the flickering firelight pushed back the darkness, Bauman began to make supper. His partner lit a torch and took a closer look at the tracks of the bad-tempered brute that had destroyed their camp.

The author introduces the problem of the story. Bigfoot has made an appearance, though unseen by the main characters (the unwelcome trappers).

When he returned to the fire, he was frowning. "Bauman," the lad observed, "that bear walked on two legs."

But Bauman just laughed. "Bears do that sometimes," he said. "Let's eat and then get some sleep. We got traps to check tomorrow and new ones to set."

After supper, their bellies full, the young trappers crawled into the lean-to, wrapped themselves in their blankets, and quickly fell asleep. 'Long about midnight, some noise or other woke Bauman up. It was then that he smelled it—a fierce wild-beast odor. Was the creature back, the one that had raided their camp? And was it planning another attack?

Bauman grabbed his rifle and fired a shot into the woods, waking his partner. They both heard something, something big, crashing into the brush as it fled. On their guard now, they built up their fire and took turns keeping watch all night, rifles ready. The creature did not return.

The next day, the lads were taking no chances. They stayed together as they checked traps and set others along the stream, traveling farther and farther upstream. As the sun began to set, tired but satisfied with their work, they headed back to camp.

What they saw took their breath away.

The lean-to was again destroyed. But this time, things were not just flung about, they were ripped to shreds and trampled on. Something was very, very angry with them. And it had left its giant tracks all over their camp.

"No man left these footprints," Bauman said as he examined them closely.

"No bear neither," his partner said grimly. "Sure, bears rear up now and then, maybe take a few steps, but this thing stayed on two feet the whole time!"

The author increases the tension. The trappers now know they are dealing with a dangerous foe.

Uneasy, the boys studied the forest that seemed to be crowding around the glade, as if it would swallow up their tiny camp. They realized they were invaders as far as this creature was concerned. It wanted them gone, that much was clear, except they couldn't leave now. So they built up their fire and huddled beside it, each lad taking a turn keeping watch, his arms wrapped protectively around his rifle.

And sure enough, 'long about midnight, that thing came back. They smelled it first, smelled its devilish odor. Then they heard it rustling about in the darkness. The boys fired off a couple of shots, hoping to hit it, but the thing just kept moving restlessly around in that impenetrable blackness, apparently afraid only of the fire. From time to time it uttered an **exasperated**, drawn-out moan.

The author creates a mood of fear. Readers are meant to feel the terror of the trappers.

At the first signs of sunlight Bauman and his partner called it quits and left camp to gather up their traps. Their plan after this was to pack up whatever was still in one piece and head out of that infernal place.

As they set out for the traps, they kept glancing anxiously about. The longer they walked, though, the more they relaxed. After all, the beast had never come after them in the daylight. They even began to whistle cheerfully as they gathered up their traps.

"Look," Bauman said to his partner. "There are only three traps left. Why don't I go get 'em while you go back and pack up. That way, we can clear out sooner and get to the ponies before dark."

The author could have had the boys leave the forest at this point in the story, but introduces a new plot development to put them in more danger (and thus keep the readers interested).

It seemed like a decent plan, so the two parted company. But Bauman found some beaver in one trap and had to skin them. He discovered that another trap had floated off and needed to track it down. It took him most of the day to do all that had to be done. It was late afternoon before he began heading back.

As the forest darkened, Bauman became uneasy. He quickened his pace, straining to pick up odd sounds, but all he heard were his feet crunching on the pine needles and his breath coming out in ragged gasps. As he neared camp, he realized he should be hearing something else—his partner packing up.

Bauman cried out hopefully but got no response. He cried out again and could hear the fear in his voice.

Dead silence.

Desperate now, he dropped his load and raced

into camp. His eyes fell on the packs, neatly wrapped, set in a pile. He noticed that the fire had been properly **extinguished**. Then he saw his partner. And the tracks. His stunned brain tried to piece together what must have happened:

After finishing his tasks in the camp, the unfortunate lad sat down on a log to wait. It rushed out of the woods then from behind him, reached out its giant arms, and broke the poor boy's neck. It had sunk its teeth into his throat but was interrupted by Bauman's return. The broken body was still warm.

Bauman let out a wail, rose, and looked wildly about. He caught a glimpse of it then, shaggy and standing tall, looking more like a man than a bear and glaring fiercely at him, as if daring him to stay where he wasn't wanted. Bauman froze, too scared to yell or pray.

Finally the creature turned and crashed into the brush.

Well, truth to tell, Bauman didn't have much reason left by then. He just grabbed his rifle and took off. Abandoned everything else—the packs, the traps, the beaver pelts. He raced down the mountainside to those two ponies, calmly munching on grass. Saddled them up and rode away, traveling without stopping until it got too dark to see. And he never looked back.

The story reaches its climax, or high point. Bauman sees the creature. Will he end up like his partner?

The author chooses to have Bigfoot spare Bauman's life. Why? Legends often contain a moral or lesson. The lesson here may be about preserving the environment and respect for wild animals' habitats.

Analyze the Characters, Setting, and Plot

- Who are the main characters in the legend?
- Who are the minor characters in the legend?
- Describe the setting for this legend.
- What are the two trappers after?
- What is the problem?
- How is the problem resolved? Or is it?
- How does the legend end?

Focus on Comprehension: Sequence of Events

- What was happening to their camp while the young men were setting traps?
- In the middle of the night, Bauman shot his rifle. What did he notice right before this?
- After retrieving most of their traps, the two trappers decided to split up. What happened to each trapper after this?

Analyze the Tools Writers Use: Mood

- Reread the opening two paragraphs. What kind of mood is the writer trying to establish in the reader's mind? Why?
- How does the author appeal to the reader's senses of sight, smell, and hearing to develop the mood?
- A forest is usually considered to be a lovely, peaceful place. How is the reader supposed to feel about the forest in this story? Explain your answer by using evidence from the text.

Focus on Words: Prefixes

Two more advanced prefixes are *circum* meaning "around" and *ex* meaning "from or out of." Words that use these prefixes are **circumvent** which means "to go around" and **exit** which means "a way out." Make a chart like the one below. Read each word in the chart. Identify the part of speech of each word as it is used in the story. Finally, explain how the prefix changes the meaning of the base word.

Page	Word	Part of speech	How the prefix changes the meaning of the base word
19	expectation		
19	expertise		
19	circumvent		
20	exhilarated		
22	circumscribed		
25	exasperated		
27	extinguished		

How does an author write a LEGEND?

Reread "Stalked by Bigfoot" and think about what Joanna Korba did to write this story. How did she develop the story? How can you, as a writer, develop your own retelling of a legend?

1. Research legends and decide on one to retell.

Most cultures have legends, so first you should decide on the culture whose legends you want to research. Look for a legend that interests you; you will do a better job retelling a legend that you like. Once you find a legend you really like, read different versions of the legend in books and from online sources. While you read these different versions, think about the parts that you will retell and the parts you will leave out.

Character	Bauman	Bauman's partner	Bigfoot
Traits	brave; bold; a bit foolhardy	hardworking; curious	angry; murderous; destructive; territorial
Examples	he thinks nothing of being in a secluded forest and he doesn't hesitate to shoot at the creature that is menacing the camp; he goes back for the three remaining traps when perhaps he and his partner should have just left the area	he does what it takes to get the job done: hikes, sets traps, and rebuilds the camp after it is destroyed; he explores the tracks left by the creature who wrecked the camp	it looks angrily at Bauman after it killed Bauman's partner and destroyed the camp several times; it doesn't want people in its habitat

2. Identify and develop characters.

Writers ask these questions:
- Who are the major and minor characters in this legend?
- What important traits does each character possess?
- What words can I use to best show these character traits?
- How do these character traits affect the plot?

3. Rethink setting and plot.

Legends, like other fiction stories, have a setting and a plot. When you write a retelling of a legend, you have to be familiar with where and when the original story takes place (the setting). You also need to be aware of the plot: the problem and events in the story, as well as the solution to the problem. Then you can choose your own words in the retelling.

Setting	The woods surrounding a river in Montana, around 1850
Problem of the Story	Two young men on a beaver-trapping expedition have their campsite destroyed by a strange creature.
Story Events	1. Bauman and his partner set their traps in a remote part of the river where a dangerous creature supposedly lives. 2. The campsite is destroyed one night, by a bear, they think. 3. The campsite is destroyed again; from the giant tracks they realize it could not have been done by a bear. 4. They decide to leave the next day—after they collect their traps. 5. Bauman spends the day collecting furs while his partner packs up the campsite. When Bauman returns to camp late in the day, he sees his partner dead and Bigfoot glaring at him.
Solution to the Problem	Bigfoot has killed Bauman's partner, but lets Bauman live. He escapes with his life, but leaves behind everything else.

Glossary

circumscribed (SER-kum-skribed) surrounded by a boundary (page 22)

circumvent (ser-kum-VENT) to follow a course around something; use wits to avoid (page 19)

euphonious (yoo-FOH-nee-us) pleasant sounding (page 11)

euphoric (yoo-FOR-ik) very happy; elated (page 11)

exasperated (ig-ZAS-puh-ray-ted) driven to anger; irritated (page 25)

exhilarated (ig-ZIH-luh-ray-ted) enlivened; excited (page 20)

expectation (ek-spek-TAY-shun) assurance that something will occur; anticipation (page 19)

expertise (ek-sper-TEEZ) skill and knowledge acquired through practice (page 19)

extinguished (ik-STIN-gwisht) stopped from burning; put out, as in a fire (page 27)

hypocritically (hih-puh-KRIH-tih-kul-lee) in dishonest contradiction to what was said; without sincerity (page 13)

hypothermia (hy-poh-THER-mee-uh) dangerously low body temperature, often caused by exposure to extreme cold (page 14)